Katarina Strömgård has illustrated—and in some cases written—over a dozen books for children. Her favorite books often inhabit the space between reality and fantasy. When she's not writing or drawing, Katarina enjoys visiting schools and libraries and holding workshops for children and adults. She lives with her family in Sweden. Visit her website at www.stromgard.com.

First published in the United States in 2019 by
Eerdmans Books for Young Readers,
an imprint of Wm. B. Eerdmans Publishing Co.
4035 Park East Court, Grand Rapids, Michigan 49546
www.eerdmans.com/youngreaders

Originally published in Sweden in 2017 under the title *En hemlig katt*

Manufactured in China

28 27 26 25 24 23 22 21 20 19   1 2 3 4 5 6 7 8 9

Library of Congress Cataloging-in-Publication Data

Names: Strömgård, Katarina, author, illustrator.
Title: The secret cat / by Katarina Strömgård.
Description: Grand Rapids MI : Eerdmans Books for Young Readers, 2019. |
Summary: Lucy yearns for a pet, so when a mysterious cat named Silvring appears one night, Lucy follows her on an amazing adventure.
Identifiers: LCCN 2018022900 | ISBN 9780802855114
Subjects: | CYAC: Adventure and adventurers—Fiction. | Cats—Fiction.
Classification: LCC PZ7.1.S7963 Sec 2019 | DDC [E]—dc23 LC record available at https://lccn.loc.gov/2018022900

The Secret Cat

Written and illustrated by

Katarina Strömgård

Eerdmans Books for Young Readers

Grand Rapids, Michigan

Some people have pets.
Others don't.
I wish I could have one.
But I'm not allowed to.

I've asked why, and Mom has given me all sorts of reasons.
They're all equally bad.
We don't have enough space in our house, she says.
And Grandma is allergic.
"We can have a beautiful aquarium full of fish instead," she offers.
But fish aren't real pets. Real pets have fur!

That night, I hear a scratching sound behind the wallpaper.
It sounds like something alive—like an animal.
Guess my name, a voice purrs through the wall.
And then I'll come to you.
"What name?" I ask.
My secret name.

I think for a few seconds,
then whisper "Silvring."

It's the type of name you have to whisper.

Then it claws open a narrow hole and slinks out.
It's a cat. A secret cat.
She rubs against me like a shadow.

Silvring is just the right size to fit in my hands.
She is perfect.
"Do you want to be my pet?" I ask.
Perhaps, she answers. *We'll see.*

I make Silvring some food—oatmeal, a banana,
and mashed potatoes.
Then Silvring wants to play with some string.
We need quite a lot of string!

Now I'd like to go outside, Silvring says.
There's not enough space here for a growing cat.

I take a closer look at Silvring. She has actually gotten bigger.
"We'd better take a leash so you don't get lost," I say.

Cats don't use leashes, says Silvring.
But we can take one along so you *don't get lost.*

There are other people out walking their pets at night.
Some of the pets are ordinary, and some of them are not.
Some of them are secret. Like Silvring.

Let's slink—as quietly as we can,
says Silvring.
Silvring likes to climb trees, and so do I.

We hide among the branches
and watch everyone below.

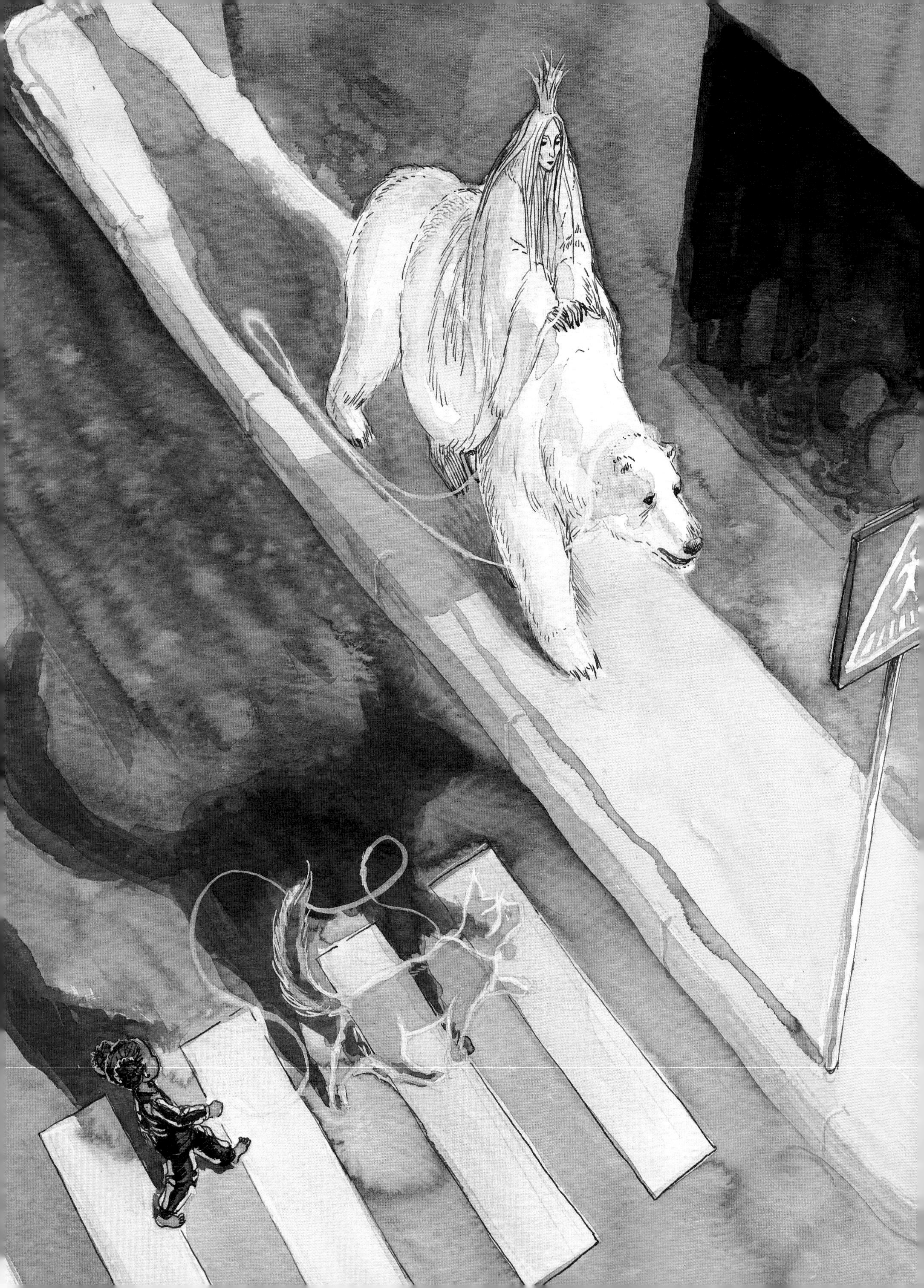

"Silvring, do you think everyone has a secret pet?" I ask.
Silvring doesn't answer. Maybe that's a secret too.
"Silvring," I say again, "Do you think all secret pets are nice?"
No, Silvring says. *Most of them are nice . . .*

. . . but some of them are dangerous.

I fling myself onto Silvring's back,
and then we run.
We run like the wind.

The Danger chases us,
but Silvring is faster.

The Danger grows larger and larger
and stretches toward us.
Silvring hisses. The Danger is huge now.

But Silvring is bigger.
So big that I can hide behind her legs,
and so strong that she can scare away anything.

Afterward, Silvring is tired and rests for a while.
She purrs when I scratch behind her ears.
You do that well. Would you like me to be your pet?
"Yes, I would," I answer. "But Mom would rather
I had fish."
I like fish, Silvring says.

Now it's time to go home, Silvring says.
"Do we have to?" I ask. I want to stay outside until the sun rises.
But Silvring doesn't answer—she's fallen asleep.

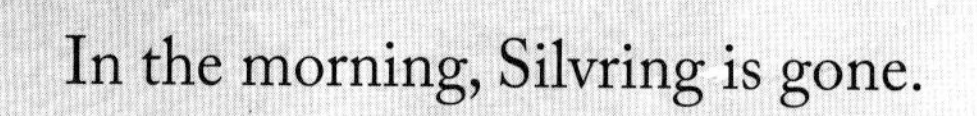

In the morning, Silvring is gone.

Everyone we see looks completely
ordinary—both the people and the pets.

Because during the day,
the secret animals sleep inside the walls,
hidden behind the wallpaper.

They sleep and wait for night to come,
and for someone to whisper:

"Silvring, come out!"